blame it on the bet

a Whiskey Sisters novel

blame it on the bet

a Whiskey Sisters novel

L.E. RICO

Entangled Publishing, LLC
2614 South Timberline Road
Suite 109
Fort Collins, CO 80525
Visit our website at www.entangledpublishing.com.

Bliss is an imprint of Entangled Publishing, LLC. For more information on our titles, visit http://www.entangledpublishing.com/category/bliss

Edited by Stacy Abrams and Jenn Mishler
Cover design by Fiona Jayde
Cover art from iStock

Manufactured in the United States of America

First Edition September 2017

Bliss
an Entangled imprint

For Pamela Marie Price Page.
A sweet and gentle soul who made this world a better place.
You will always be missed. You will always be loved.

Chapter One

The paper is thick and creamy, the typeface a perfectly neat and neutral Times New Roman. I've examined documents like this hundreds of times, but I'm having a hard time wrapping my head around what I'm looking at as I flip through page after page of legalese. I mean, I am, after all, a lawyer. I understand the terms. I understand the law behind the terms. What I don't understand is how these terms of the law came to apply to my father. Or, more accurately, to his estate.

"And you found this *where*?" I ask my sister Jameson.

"At home. In Pops's sock drawer. We were packing up some of his clothes to bring to the Goodwill, and there it was, in a file folder."

"Well, I guess that explains why we didn't come across it with the rest of his files in the office," I mutter.

It's been about a month now since my father was felled by a massive aneurysm, and I'm still reeling. We all are. These things, by nature, happen quickly—no symptoms, no warning.

No chance to say good-bye. Pops was dead before he hit the floor, and all I've been able to think about since then is what I should've said. What I should've done. Because here I am with a head full of memories, a heart full of regrets, and a hand full of papers that reduce his life's work to a few paragraphs of legalese.

We thought the pub was free and clear. Our parents paid off the mortgage when I was a kid. But apparently—unbeknownst to my three sisters and me—our father had been borrowing against the equity in the business. Now, as I sit at my sister's table examining the particulars of his loan activity, I see the cost of our lives unfold before me. Ten thousand here, thirty thousand there. Each five-figure withdrawal coinciding with a major life event for one of us. I see what can only be my law school tuition…and the cash he gave me to get settled in the Twin Cities. I'm comparing the math and the dates that match Jameson's nursing degree and subsequent wedding. Then there's tuition for my sister Walker and braces for Bailey. There's also a substantial withdrawal dating back to a little over a year ago, when Pops insisted on paying for his first grandchild's nursery. In all, it's more than a hundred thousand dollars.

"Holy. Crap." I flip from page to page, shaking my head in disbelief. "How did this happen? Why wouldn't he tell us?"

"Because he was a proud man, Henny," Jameson says. "He'd never ask you to take out a school loan. And he'd sooner have died than let the Clarke family pay for my wedding. And then when little Jackson was born…"

Before she can even finish her sentence, Baby Satan is in action. I don't even see the wonton as it comes hurtling across the table, hitting my cheek and sliding down my neck. It leaves a slimy trail before it splats to the floor. I can't move. None of us can. Bailey is the first to laugh. She slaps one hand over her mouth and points to me with the other, howling behind her fingers. Walker is right there with her, trying desperately not to spit her mouthful of wine all over the table. Jameson is the only one who is not amused.

"Jackson Winston Clarke!" she shrieks at my nephew, the dumpling-flinger.

His entire little body is shaking with a deep belly laugh, and he's already reaching into his Winnie the Pooh bowl for something else to toss my way.

"Win!" Jameson calls over her shoulder. *"Wiiiiiiiiiiiiiiin!"*

"What the hell, James? Dad and I are trying to watch *Jeopardy!,*" my jerk of a brother-in-law says when he deigns to enter the kitchen where my three sisters and I are all sitting around the table, eating Chinese takeout.

Oh, he's handsome, all right. Win Jr. is your typical Minnesota hottie—tall, blond-haired, and blue-eyed. But the attractive qualities stop there.

"Win, Jackson is done with his dinner. Please take him up and give him his bath. I'll come and tuck him in when you're done," my sister instructs, hauling the little felon out of his highchair and holding him out toward his father...who's already shaking his head.

"No, no, no. Sorry, James, but I'm beat. I've had a long day, and I'm in no mood..."

He stops as soon as she gives him "the look." The one that says "do this now, or you'll pay for it later." I know that look very well, and judging by how quickly Win snatches his son from his wife's arms, he does, too. I can still hear him grumbling under his breath as I swab the remnants of the wonton from my cleavage.

Walker is still snickering as she pulls the guts out of an egg roll.

"I'm so sorry, Hennessy," Jameson apologizes as she kneels to wipe the food from the floor. When she looks up at me, I can see the dark circles under her moss-colored eyes and…could that be the start of crow's feet? God, Jameson's only twenty-five, a year-and-a-half younger than me, but you wouldn't know that to look at her. Even her beautiful auburn hair seems tired, pulled back into a wilted ponytail. I reach down and put a hand on her shoulder.

"It's not a big deal, really. He's just excited to see me. It's been a while since his favorite aunt was in town."

"Oh, puh-leeeeeeease." Seventeen-year-old Bailey groans as she rolls her perfect blue eyes and tosses her perfectly straight, perfectly golden-blonde tresses. "If anyone's Jackson's favorite, it's me. I'm the one who babysits…"

"Yeah, well, you're not my favorite," Jameson chimes in, returning to her own seat. "You're the one who lets him eat enough sugary crap to keep him up for twenty-four hours straight."

"I haven't got all night, you know," grumbles Walker, suddenly less amused and more irritated. "Can we please just get on with it already?"

It's been a long-ass day, and I'm tired—exhausted, really—and I have no patience for Walker's signature snark.

"You know," I begin, dropping my voice and leaning across the table toward her, "I had to convince my boss to give me some time off—and right in the middle of a big case. I threw a few things into a bag and drove the three hours up here because you guys said something was really wrong and that you needed me. So, here I am—and don't you dare tell me you've got 'stuff to do,' Walker."

"Hennessy's right," Jameson says soothingly. She's good at that, calming the ever-churning tension among the four of us. "She dropped everything because we asked her to come. The least we can do is show a little gratitude."

Walker's turn to roll her eyes. Unlike the blue and green shared by most of our family, hers are the color of gray flannel.

"Fine," she spits. "Because, you know, the earth doesn't

spin without Hennessy O'Halloran. And, just for the record, *I* thought we could sort it out on our own."

Jameson is rubbing her temples now, and I can see she needs this like a hole in the head. I've got to get this thing back on the rails, or we'll be here all night long. I draw in a long, deep breath and take another stab at diplomacy.

"Guys, let's not do this. Please. Look, I'm here now, and we can get the business back on track. I'll take over the day-to-day of the pub. James, maybe you can handle the paperwork? Walker, we all know you're the best bartender in the family, after Pops. You can help out nights and weekends when you're not in school. And Bailey can help in the kitchen and with serving food. I'll call the bank tomorrow and see if I can refinance the loan. That should buy us a couple of months—"

"Hennessy." Jameson cuts me off. "We don't have a couple of months."

This time, she takes a letter from the drawer of the sideboard and hands it to me. I pull it from its envelope and start to read, my jaw dropping a little lower with every line that I skim. I glance, more than once, between the official correspondence and Jameson's drawn face.

"What?" I gasp, not believing what's right there in black in white. "They're calling the loan? The bank is calling the entirety of the loan? And they want it in…*ninety* days?"

"That's not the worst of it," Jameson says solemnly. "Keep reading."

She's right. Upon further inspection, I see that this is the *second* notice. I look at the date at the top of the page and do the math in my head. Six weeks. We've already lost six weeks, and there are only six more to go.

Oh my God. Oh my God. Oh my God.

"How?" I whisper.

Jameson shrugs slightly and shakes her head. "I don't know. Maybe the first notice was lost in the mail. Maybe it was somehow shredded with the rest of Pops's paperwork. But, however it happened, we're in a pretty tight spot here."

"You can fix it, though, right, Henny?" Bailey asks hopefully from across the table.

I consider her closely. Not even out of high school and she's lost both parents. She lives at home with Walker, who's rarely there, and depends on a hot meal from the woman we pay to clean up the house, shop, and make dinner most nights. At least the rest of us are adults, more or less. The last thing Bailey needs is to be worried about something like this.

"I'm going to try, Bailey," I say with the most reassuring smile that I can muster. "I just have to figure out where to begin…"

"Well, this might help," Jameson says, reaching into the sideboard once more.

"God, James!" I huff. "Another one? Quit the drama already, and just give me everything at one time, will you?"

She scowls.

"This is the last one. And excuse me for trying to break it to you gently. We've all had a few days to digest this."

I don't respond as I take the last document from her hand. It's a letter of intent to purchase the pub property. Upon closer examination, I see that it's come from a real estate developer out of Los Angeles—some guy named Bryan Truitt has made an offer to purchase the pub, and by the looks of this, my father was planning to accept. I'm suddenly struck by how little I knew about what was going on here. I was so busy trying to prove to myself and everybody else that I could make it in the "Big City," that I was oblivious to what was unfolding back here at home.

"All righty, then. It would appear we have a little mystery to unravel if we hope to salvage the pub," I say with quiet resignation as I let go of the paper and watch it waft down past the table, landing on the oak floor in my sister's dining room with a soft *swoosh*. "And I suspect this Bryan Truitt guy is at the center of it."

• • •

It takes me a few seconds to locate the key on my ring. And, when I finally do manage to get it into the lock, I have to jiggle it a little before the deadbolt retracts. It's been a while since anyone has used the apartment above the pub. The steep, narrow staircase is dark. I reach for the light, but nothing happens when I flip the switch. I leave my suitcase at the bottom of the stairs, propping open the door with it so I can have a slice of light from the streetlamp outside. The upstairs lock is considerably smoother than the downstairs one, and when I reach around on the wall, I find the light switch, and the apartment's interior hall light comes on. Perfect.

Once I reclaim my suitcase and hoist it up the stairs to join me, I close the door behind me. I heave a deep sigh and take a long, appraising look at the tiny rooms that were our home for the first seven years of my life. It was sweet, and cozy, and I loved sharing a room with James. But then, along came Walker, and my parents shoehorned her crib in between Jameson's and my beds. By the time Bailey came a few years later, it was clear that the O'Halloran Clan needed something bigger. That's when we moved to the little cape cod on Orange Avenue.

Like the rest of the place, the bedroom smells musty. Clearly no one's stayed here since I was in town for my father's funeral in December. I crack open the windows on the opposite side of the room, inhaling the frigid, fresh air.

Back in the kitchen, I get a K-Cup going in the Keurig and pull the phone out of my pocket. The phone that I've been ignoring all night.

There are a few messages from work that I'll return

tomorrow, and twice that number of work-related emails. Several un-work-related emails offer me a hot Russian beauty, an all-natural miracle for erectile dysfunction, and a walk-in tub.

And then there's the text. Just the one.

Hey. You get there okay?

That's from my "Friend with Benefits," who shall remain nameless. Because I like it that way. And so does he. This relationship couldn't get any more casual. We were random strangers in a bar who found out after last call that we lived in the same apartment building. We decided to share more than the Uber ride home. It's not love or anything. It's not even lust—not for me, at least. FWB has come in very handy during the long, dark winter nights. Oh, who the hell am I kidding? The *lonely* winter nights. Well, at least he cares enough to check on me, and that's something. He's also agreed to water my plants while I'm gone. My thumbs are a blur as I text him a succinct reply.

All good, TYVM. TTYL.

I flop onto the couch and close my eyes. It's good to be home—even under these insane circumstances. It's been a long time since I've lived here in Mayhem—college, law school, and my internship having kept me downstate. Finally, the pot of gold at the end of that particular rainbow was an assistant district attorney position with the Hennepin County Prosecutor's office.

The truth is that I could have had Jameson send me all the papers—hell, I could've asked one of the senior partners to go over them with me. But I packed up and got in my car before I'd even gotten off the phone with her, calling the office from the road.

What's wrong with me?

I've got a good job, and I make decent—if not great—money. My overpriced apartment has a nice view of the Mississippi River and a sexy, hot, anonymous guy on the next floor up. What have I got to be unhappy about? It's ridiculous.

I rub my temples, trying to push back the dull ache that's starting to surface. That's when I spot the framed pictures of us on the mantel. My father's broad, easy smile shines back at me.

"What happened, Pops?" I ask the silence. "And how can I make it right?"

The silence has no reply.

Chapter Two

BRYAN

Truittism Number 2: Nothing is better than "boots on the ground" to properly assess an unclear situation.

The sun is in my eyes. It slips through the crack of space where the blinds end and the windowsill begins, stealthily creeping across the carpeted floor, seeking out the delicate tissue of my eyelids. This is why I have special blackout blinds and an added layer of insulated drapes in my bedroom. Unfortunately, I'm not in my bedroom. I know this because I feel the coarse grain leather of my office couch under my face.

I try to turn so that I'm facing the back cushions, but my body seems to be stuck, all six foot two of me wedged into the five feet of space between armrests. All I can do is squeeze my eyes shut against the burning glare. It makes my eyelids look red, even when they're closed. I groan in frustration, wanting nothing more than to just fall back to sleep. Suddenly, my world goes blissfully dark again. Something has inserted itself between the sun and me, like a beautiful eclipse. Did the blinds somehow drop all the way down? Did my desk somehow silently flip over onto its side? Maybe it really is an eclipse. Or a rogue asteroid.

Turns out it's not a what, but a who. Helen.

"W-What are you doing here?" I mutter hoarsely.

"I work here," my assistant says tartly as she looks down upon me with undisguised disdain. "It smells like a brewery in here," she informs me. "And a locker room. Like the locker room of a brewery," she pronounces with a disapproving *tsk* of her tongue.

"Huh," is all I can manage, allowing my eyes to close again. But then she moves away, and I writhe like a vampire burned by the brightening dawn. Is that my flesh I smell burning?

"You have a perfectly lovely condo," Helen says as she unfolds a white plastic trash bag. "I don't understand why you feel the need to sleep here." When she jerks the bag open with a loud *snap*, I wince.

"Please. Could you please, please, please keep it down?"

But she ignores me, chattering away as she moves around my office, tossing takeout containers and beer bottles into the bag. I can't make out everything she's saying, but I catch a word here and there. Something about my hedonistic lifestyle catching up with me someday.

"Why are you here so early?" I grumble. "And what are you doing?"

She stops and looks at me, one garish orange eyebrow quirked.

"Uh, well, let's see…I'm cleaning up this pigsty that you call an office. Once I've gotten all the trash and beer bottles out of the way, I'm going to bring in a guy with a power washer to see if we can't get the smell out of the walls. But I'm not holding out hope."

I decide to ignore her and close my eyes again. But a few

seconds later I experience a hellish glare. Helen's opened the blinds all the way, and the sun is now streaming in, washing my wilted body in the unwanted light of day.

"Oh, come on, Helen…" I say. "I'm trying to sleep here!"

She comes and stands over me again, peering at me over the blue-framed glasses, the ones that dangle from a chain around her neck when she doesn't need them. From this angle, her bright orange hair is particularly puffy. She reminds me of one of those troll dolls. The ones that are kind of cute and creepy at the same time.

"Bryan, it's after nine. You have to get up. I brought you a change of clothes and your shaving kit."

I struggle to sit up, my hand acting as a visor until my heavy eyes can adjust to the light. Ugh. I feel like I've been hit with a bag filled with rocks. No…something bigger. Hammers, maybe. Yeah, great big hammers. Sledgehammers.

"You let yourself into my place? How the hell did you know I wouldn't be there? I might have been…you know… *entertaining*."

Helen scoffs and rolls her watery blue eyes.

"Please. There aren't even sheets on your bed. In fact, there's nothing in that apartment. Not a painting on the wall, not a framed picture. You have exactly one set of dishes and silverware for four. But there's no food in the fridge, and your oven still has the plastic cling label from when you bought it."

With some difficulty, I haul myself to my feet so I'm now looking down on the troll doll.

"Helen, how I live is none of your business," I hiss with an accompanying glare. But she's unmoved. Clearly I'm not as menacing as I'd like to think. Finally I roll my eyes and go into the small private bathroom in the back of my office. When I get in there, I find a freshly dry-cleaned suit, clean underwear and socks, and my toiletries. After a hot shower and shave, I dress and comb back my damp hair before taking a look in the full-length mirror mounted on the back of the door.

"That's better," I murmur, taking note of the dark circles under my bloodshot eyes.

When I come back out into my office, I find a steaming hot latte on my desk along with a bowl of…what *is* that?

"It's oatmeal," Helen says from the doorway when she sees me scowling down at the grayish mush. "You need something hot and substantial. There's also a cup of fresh berries there."

I sink into the very expensive ergonomic chair behind my desk with a loud grunt. Once upon a time, I would only hire assistants of the leggy, blonde variety. And, while they made for some lovely scenery around the office, none of these women had any actual administrative experience. They were all models and actresses and screenwriters just waiting to be "discovered." It was a mess all around. And then came Helen.

Five minutes into her job interview I'd pretty much decided to add her to the "don't call us, we'll call you" pile. Then she did something very interesting. She pointed out there was a stain on my tie. Who does that? Who risks pissing off—or, worse yet, embarrassing the person who's conducting your job interview? Helen. That's who. It was right then and there that I realized she was *exactly* what I needed. A no-nonsense woman who wasn't afraid to speak her mind, no matter what was at stake. An assistant who would always have my back. I've never regretted that decision. Except for maybe now as she eyeballs me with a mixture of pity and concern.

"Thank you for the breakfast," I say, gesturing to the low-cholesterol feast on my desk. "And the clothes. I appreciate it."

She nods curtly.

"I know. If you didn't, I wouldn't." She comes to take a seat in front of my desk. "Now, let's go over your schedule for the day—"

"Uh-uh." I interrupt her, shaking my head as I spoon some oatmeal into my mouth.

Damn, it's actually good.

"The highest priority today is the Minnesota property," I say. "I pitched it to Cinecore six months ago, and they want to know why the acquisition is taking so long."

"Still nothing from the owner? What's his name... O'Halloran?"

I nod. "Jack O'Halloran. He was in. We only had to sign the final papers, and then he just dropped off the face of the earth. I'm guessing he got cold feet."

"Yeah, I might get cold feet, too, if I were doing business with you," Helen mutters under her breath, but she continues before I can comment. "All right. How would you like to proceed, then?"

That's the other thing I like about Helen—she gets right down to business.

I tap a few keys to wake up my computer and then scan my emails. Still no response from the owner of O'Halloran's Pub. Well, this is his unlucky day because I'm done playing nice. We had a gentleman's agreement, and I'm about done being a gentleman.

"I'm going to give him a call. If I can't get an answer out of him—or if he decides to hide like a chicken—then I'll have to take matters into my own hands."

"So, it's a possible Truittism Number Two then?" she asks with raised eyebrows.

I grin from ear to ear. Yes, Helen was a brilliant hire. She's memorized my entire litany of truisms, or Truittisms, as I like to call them.

"Exactly."

"All right, I'll leave you to it, then. Let me know what I can do to help. Meanwhile, I'll be at my desk answering the messages that came in overnight."

Once she's closed the door, I pull out the file and open it on my desk. There are pictures of the property, along with copies of the deed, Certificates of Occupancy, and a ream of banking and loan records that I shouldn't have…but do. I've spent a lot of time cultivating a network of "spies" all over the country. When one of them spots an available property—or a property that's about to become available—he or she contacts me. If the lead pans out, there's a nice finder's fee involved for them. This pub in the tiny town of Mayhem is a perfect fit for one of my projects, and I have no intention of losing it at the eleventh hour.

I pick up the phone on my desk and punch in the number listed in the file, and within a few seconds, a telephone is ringing somewhere in the middle of the country. Once. Twice. Three times.

"O'Halloran's," an impatient female voice barks at me across two time zones.

"With whom am I speaking, please?" I keep my tone brusque and businesslike.

"This is Walker."

Funny, I thought Walker was a guy's name. Maybe I didn't hear her right.

"I'm sorry, did you say *Walker*?" And then I just can't help myself. "Like *Walker, Texas Ranger*?"

"Hah! That's so hilarious," she replies in a tone that is anything but amused. "'Cause, you know, I've never heard that one before. What else you got? Luke Skywalker, maybe? Or one of those zombie things from *The Walking Dead*? Go ahead, I've got all day," she snarls down the line.

Suddenly I'm not feeling so clever anymore. I clear my throat and start again.

"Sorry about that. I was actually calling to speak with Jack O'Halloran, please."

There's a long pause.

"And who did you say you are?" She sounds suspicious all of a sudden.

"My name is Bryan Truitt, of The Truitt Group in Los Angeles."

Another long pause before I get a chilly response.

"I see. Well, sorry, but he's not available."

"Okay, can you tell me when he *will* be available?" I persist. "I've been trying to reach him for some time."

"I'm sorry, but you'll need to take it up with the manager. That would be Hennessy."

"Hennessy?"

"Hennessy."

"Is Hennessy there now?"

"No. I'm here."

"And you're not Hennessy."

"No, I already told you. I'm Walker."

"So when is a good time to call back?"

"Look, Mr. Pruitt…"

"Truitt. It's *Truitt.*"

"Fine. Whatever. Just give me your number, and I'll leave a message."

No way I'm letting this go now that I've got a real live human being on the line.

"I'm sorry, but I'm not prepared to do that," I inform her coolly.

"Suit yourself. Call back when you *are* prepared to do that. Until then, you're not speaking to anyone. Including me."

An earful of dial tone assaults me before I can object.

"What just happened?" I mutter, still staring at the phone in my hand.

I sit back in my chair and close my eyes, breathing in for five counts, then out for five counts. In, out. In, out, until I feel my blood pressure drop. My therapist calls it "square breathing" or some nonsense like that. But I have to hand it to her, it works.

In. Out. In. Out…

Oh to hell with this.

"Helen!" I bellow.

In three seconds flat, my door flies open and short, squat Helen is standing in the doorway. "Did I give you the impression that I'm hard of hearing?"

"Sorry," I mutter, pulling a bottle of aspirin from my desk drawer and pouring a few directly into my mouth, chasing them with a gulp of coffee. "I need you to clear my schedule for the rest of the week and make travel plans for me."

She nods, making a note on her pad. "Where?"

"Mayhem, Minnesota."

Helen looks up at me.

"Where?"

"Mayhem. It's in Minnesota."

"That's a place?"

"Apparently. I have no idea how to get there. You'll have to figure that out. It'd be great if you could get me on the first plane out tomorrow."

"Return ticket for when?"

"I don't know yet. Depends on how long it takes me to get what I want."

Helen snorts and rolls her eyes. "So, tomorrow night, then?"

"You know it. There's a reason they call the Midwest 'fly-over country.'" I grin. "Nothing there worth landing for."

"Apparently there's something worth landing for, or you wouldn't want 'boots on the ground.' Speaking of which, would you like me to go pick up a few cold-weather wardrobe items before you go? Winter coat, boots, gloves, that kind of thing?"

"Nope. I don't plan on being there long enough to need them."

She raises an eyebrow. "Seriously? You think you'll be able to get this sale squared away that quick?"

"That's what I'm hoping."

"Well, if you're sure… You know the temperature can drop below zero this time of year, don't you?"

In the beginning, I used to find this kind of conversation irritating because I thought Helen was questioning my judgment or my ability…or, at times, my sanity. But I've since come to realize that she has genuine concern for my wellbeing. Something I still find a little foreign…but not altogether unpleasant.

"I can have something waiting for you on that end if you don't want to haul a coat on the plane with you," she adds.

"Thanks, but I really am hoping to be in and out in under twenty-four hours."

"All righty, then," she says, jotting down a few notes on her pad. "You just do whatever you think is best. "

Oh. I plan to.

Chapter Three

"The Whiskey Sisters."

That's what the four of us have been called for as long as I can remember. Never in a derogatory way, though—it was always a sweet term of endearment used by our friends and neighbors. But it was more than a nod to the names our parents chose for us—it was about our relationship to the business itself. "Every O'Halloran has a stake in O'Halloran's," our father would tell us. And he wasn't kidding.

I was drafted to wash dishes when I turned fifteen. Jameson got to file Pops's paperwork. Walker learned the ins and outs of mixology long before she was old enough to drink. Even Bailey spent her summer vacations serving fish and chips to the tourists passing through town. It was a family business in the truest sense of the word.

After a fitful night's sleep in my childhood bedroom, I dress and slip down the rear staircase—the one that goes from the apartment kitchen into the back corridor of the pub, where my father's office and the kitchen are. When we were kids, my mother would send us down that way to kiss our father good night.

Everything is dark and still when I open the door at the bottom of the stairs. It'll be another hour yet before Donovan comes in to prep for lunch, so I've got the whole place to myself. I head into my father's office without bothering to flip the switch that illuminates the small, narrow hallway. I know it's exactly eighteen paces from here. I know that I need to lift the door just a hair so it doesn't catch on the frame. And I know the switch to my left will light the small lamp on Pops's desk. With a deep sigh, I sit down in his wooden desk chair on wheels, the kind that they stopped manufacturing years ago because the base was unstable.

Sitting at the back edge of the calendar/blotter are framed pictures of us all. Mama and Pops on their wedding day. My high school graduation. James's wedding to the dipstick. Bailey's sweet sixteen. My favorite, by far, is a picture of Pops, sound asleep on Jameson's couch, with a teeny, tiny Jackson also asleep, right atop Pops's chest. I pick up the silver frame and rub a thumb across the image of my father's face, so peaceful and content with his first grandson.

When the rage bubbles up from somewhere deep inside, I am totally unprepared. It seems to come out of nowhere. My chest and neck and face grow hot in stages, and I'm sure I must look like a thermometer with its mercury rising higher and higher. Hot tears sting my eyes and threaten to spill down my cheeks. My breath comes in short, raspy pants, and I have to jump up to my feet. I pace the room, my hands raking through my long, thick hair. It's as if I'm going to come right out of my skin.

Pant. Pant. Pant.

Pace. Pace. Pace.

So many memories missed. So much time lost.

I've been such a fool.

The five words hit me like brutal slaps across the face. My head actually turns to one side instinctively, as if to avoid the blows. But they keep coming.

Such a damned fool.

I'm vaguely aware of the huffing sound that I'm making. My heart feels as if it's going to pound right out of my chest, and my heated skin quickly turns cool and damp with sweat. I know this feeling. This is a panic attack. But I'm helpless to stop the cycle once it's started. I pace in circles and pant, waiting helplessly for the deep-seated accusations to float to the surface of my subconscious.

I didn't want to be a lawyer. I never wanted to be a lawyer.

I gasp and immediately stop pacing so I can bend at the waist and plant my palms on my thighs.

Breathe, Hennessy. Breathe.

Slowly…

Okay. I'm okay.

I went to law school to please my father.

I gulp back a cry that threatens to rise from my throat, but I can't keep the tears at bay any longer, and they slide in long, salty tracks down my face.

I didn't want to leave home…but I did.

My next breath is difficult to take against the tightening of my lungs and chest.

I didn't want to move away. I didn't want the job.

"Oh…God…" I groan miserably and force myself to sit down again. It's there. It's all right there, just under the surface, where it's been for more years than I'd care to admit. I was the dutiful child, fulfilling her father's dream of a better life in a big city, where I could be more than just the daughter of the local pub owners. But that's exactly who I was. Who I still am. And no amount of money, no flashy car, no swank apartment is ever going to change that.

"I'm sorry, Pops," I whisper to my father's picture on the desk as I swipe at my tears. "I'm so sorry. I never wanted to disappoint you. But I'm so lonely. I'm so unhappy."

The tears have morphed into a wash down my face now, and the only thing left to do is lay my head atop my arms on the desk and sob. And then something strange happens. My mother's voice echoes from somewhere in the dark recesses of my memory.

"Cradle to grave, Hennessy," she says after I've had a fight with Jameson over a Barbie. "Your sisters are the only ones who will be with you from the time you're born to the time you die. Not me. Not Pops. Not Grandma Elsie. Not your best friend or even the man you'll marry someday. So you must stick together—not fall apart. Do you understand me, Henny?"

I'd nodded but still pouted in my mind, unable to grasp this concept at ten years old. But I'm not ten anymore.

I sit up straight, pluck a wad of tissues out of a box on the desk, and blow my nose in a most unfeminine manner. Then I take a long, slow, shaky breath, wipe my eyes, and start opening drawers and rummaging through filing cabinets. I pore over ledgers and inspect invoices.

It takes hours. I stay holed up in the office, no one even aware of my presence there in the back of the pub. I plow through the countless tiny, intricate jigsaw pieces until I finally have a clear understanding of just how deep of a pile of crap we're standing in. Except, it's more of a mountain than a pile, and by the time I return the last bank statement to the last file folder and close the last desk drawer, I know the depths to which my father went to provide for and protect his girls.

"There you are! I've been looking all over for you!" Jameson says from the doorway. I didn't even hear her open the door. "Hey! Hey, hey...what is it? You've been crying!" She's kneeling down next to my chair in a heartbeat, taking my hands in hers and searching my eyes for a clue.

"I'm okay now. Really," I reassure her with a weak smile. "Pull up that stool and come sit with me. I've been going through Pops's papers…"

"But we've been through all of those already, Henny. There isn't anything there…"

"Yes, there is. Not alone, but when you put it all together, you can see the pattern. You can tell where things start to go wrong and how Pops tried to make it right. But he couldn't. By the time he got involved with this Truitt person, he must have been desperate."

She looks at me, her green eyes widening with comprehension.

"Wait—what are you saying? Pops knew Truitt? I thought he came into the picture after the bank called the loan. You know, to try and scoop up the property for pennies on the dollar."

"I don't think so," I say softly. "Pops was desperate to leave something for us. And, more importantly, he didn't want to be a financial burden on any of his children. He was going to sell, James."

"No!" she squeaks in protest. "Pops would never do that! This…" She gestures at the room around us. "This was his life. His and Mama's."

"I'd like to believe he was railroaded or blackmailed into it, but if you follow the money, you'll see that it was the only option he could find. Jesus, no wonder he had an aneurysm. His blood pressure must've been through the roof! Did you notice anything?"

She looks stunned as she pulls up the stool in the corner and sits so we're eye-to-eye.

"He…he was preoccupied, I suppose. A little forgetful, maybe? Especially in the fall…"

I pick up the papers from The Truitt Group and wave them around.

"And that's exactly when all this was happening. Near as I can tell, Truitt had some inside information that the pub was in trouble. He reached out to Pops and expressed an interest in the business."

"So he *is* a predator," she says with some satisfaction.

For me, it's not so cut and dry.

"Maybe, in that he had Pops over a barrel. But honestly, he didn't try to undercut him. In fact, near as I can tell, he was offering full fair-market value on the pub. Pops would have walked away debt-free with a good chunk of change in his pocket."

We stare at one another silently for a very long, very awkward moment.

"So…" she begins. "What does that mean?"

I sigh.

"I think it means that Pops saw selling as a way to avoid the embarrassment of foreclosure…and a way to avoid letting on to us just how much debt he was in. He probably intended to play it off as being his plan all along. And by then, there wouldn't be anything any of us could have done about it, anyway. But now he's gone, and we know the whole story. And, just maybe, we can still do something to turn this thing around."

My sister is nodding, her face solemn as she processes what I'm saying.

"So, this isn't just about money anymore," Jameson observes.

"No," I agree. "It's about pride. His pride…and ours."

Chapter Four

BRYAN

Truittism Number 3: Don't judge a book by its cover…or its title.

It's taken me the entire day to get to this godforsaken speck on the map. Three flights and one harrowing drive through the Arctic Circle later, I pull into the town of Mayhem, Minnesota. What a name.

The first thing that strikes me is the snow.

This is not the snow of film and television—light, fluffy, glittery flakes of goodness that serenely float down from the heavens. The snow I see now is heaped into scuzzy piles in parking lots, against buildings, and lining the sidewalks like filthy, muddy icebergs. This snow is pocked and scarred from rock salt. It's dirty from sand and grime. This is not angelic snow. This is angry snow. Snow with an attitude.

"Ugh." I scowl at it in disgust as I maneuver my rented Lexus sedan down Main Street.

I have no trouble spotting the pub, and I'm happy to find a clear spot to park directly across the street from the quaint two-story building. The building that I should own by now. I take a deep breath and put on my game face. Expensive car. Impeccably tailored suit. Hand-tooled, leather-soled Italian dress shoes. An Armani trench and a buttery leather briefcase. As I open the door and step out onto the street, I'm ready to make an impression Jack O'Halloran will never forget.

I cross the street, careful not to step in any slushy puddles, but when I get to the curb, I'm faced with a dilemma. Some genius has neglected to shovel a path through the stacked snow between the road and the sidewalk. I can either go over the three-foot mound or walk to the end of the block and come back around from the corner.

"Oh screw it," I mutter, clutching my briefcase tightly and stepping up high to hoist myself over the berm.

No sooner does my foot land than it sinks, the snow beneath it giving way under my weight and leaving me with one leg embedded up to the thigh while the other dangles behind me. I grumble under my breath and try to extricate myself without falling forward or backward—I'm balancing precariously between the two. Except that my left leg—the free leg—doesn't quite reach the asphalt, so I don't have anything to push against for leverage in order to pull my right one out of its icy prison.

"What the—"

"Hey, you all right?" comes a female voice at close range.

I've been focusing so hard on this conundrum that I didn't even notice I have an audience. Great. Just what I need, some local yokel come to gawk at the townie.

"I'm fine, I'm fine," I mutter, trying, unsuccessfully, to yank myself free. I grunt in disgust at the bottom of my Armani trench, which is now covered in filth from dragging along this iceberg that has absorbed a quarter of my body. "Oh hell…"

"Funny, you don't look fine."

I tear myself away from my current predicament to examine the smart-ass on the sidewalk. I don't know what I'm expecting to see, but she's not it.

The woman I'm looking at is, quite simply, gorgeous. Like, heart-stoppingly beautiful. And the funny thing is, she's not like the women I'm usually drawn to. This is the *real* girl next door. She's dressed in jeans, her arms folded across the plaid flannel shirt she's wearing over a tee that reads *O'Halloran's Pub*. On her feet are a pair of boots—and I'm not talking about those tall, leather, spiky-heeled boots that women teeter around on in L.A. These are *boot* boots. Like the functional kind with navy blue rubber-bottoms and brown leather uppers that lace up high on her shins. Tufts of warm lining peek out around the collars.

Her hair is dirty blond, hanging down around her face in a messy tumble of untamed curls and waves. There's an arc of freckles dotting the bridge of her slightly upturned nose, and her eyes are the brightest blue I think I've ever seen.

Wow.

I'm so busy looking that I've actually stopped hearing, and I have the uncomfortable feeling that she's just asked me a question.

"Excuse me?"

"I asked if you're hurt," she informs me as she wipes her hands on a half-apron wrapped around her waist.

"What? Oh no. No…just my pride," I say with a sheepish grin. "I appear to be stuck."

"So I see."

"I…I guess I should've gone around to the corner instead of trying to climb Everest here," I kid.

"I suppose you should have," she says with a smirk. "Would you like some help, maybe?"

Hmmm. On the one hand, I'm embarrassed. On the other,

I'll get to touch this snow bunny. Oh yeah. Plan B it is.

"That would be great," I say, offering up my most sincere, earnest smile. "Would you mind taking this for me?"

I hold my leather briefcase out, and she comes forward to take it from me. There, that's better. Now I can use both hands to…to what?

"Here," she says, coming closer and turning to her side. "Put a hand on my shoulder and see if that gives you enough leverage to pull your foot out."

She doesn't have to suggest it twice. I put a hand on her delicate frame and try to extricate myself. Unfortunately, the only thing I succeed in doing is sinking my other foot into the snow bank—though, not nearly as deep. That's when I feel strong hands around my waist, pulling me backward. And up. And out. My feet slip and slide—first against the snow, and then on the slick road.

"Whoa! Hey…!"

"Hold on there, son, I've got you," a deep voice says from behind me. Once I'm stable again, I feel his grip on me relax, and turn to thank the Good Samaritan, already speaking as I do.

"Thanks, man, I was good and stuck there… *Jesus Christ!*" I gasp in surprise, startled to find myself staring at a very tall, imposing figure. He's got dark hair and eyes, and he's wearing all black. That is, except for his white collar. A priest's collar. He throws his head back in a loud laugh that echoes on the pavement and down the quiet block.

"Not quite, son, but you're getting warmer!" he howls at my exclamation.

I think I've stepped into a David Lynch film.

"I–I'm sorry, I…I didn't mean to be offensive, Father…I was just…" The words tumble out of my mouth and he just smiles at me kindly, clearly amused.

"Tell you what," he says, taking me by the elbow and

guiding me around a patch of black ice, "let's you and I take a walk around onto the nice salted and sanded sidewalk, shall we?"

I nod and allow myself to be led down and back around until we're standing in front of the pub. In front of the hottie. She looks down at my hand-tooled Italian leather loafers, then back up at me again.

"I know those are some spendy shoes," she comments, "but you might want to get yourself a pair of boots if you're going to be in town for more than a day or two. Otherwise, you're likely to do a header every time you hit a slick patch."

Spendy?

"Ah, thanks," I reply, feeling unexpectedly—and uncomfortably—nervous.

What the hell is *that* about?

"I don't plan to be in town more than a night or two. I live in Los Angeles, and there's not much call for snow boots there…"

Something in her smooth, delicate features changes, hardens. Her brow furrows just a touch.

"I'm Bryan Truitt," I say, stepping forward to offer her my hand.

Now the brows go up as if she recognizes me. Or my name. Before I can ascertain whether or not that's the case, the priest jumps in.

"Aha! I didn't think you were from around these parts. Much too tan, don't you know." He chuckles. "What is it that brings you to Mayhem, Mr. Truitt?"

"Please, call me Bryan. Uh…I'm here to see a guy by the name of Hennessy. Hennessy O'Halloran. I think he's maybe managing the pub here…" I gesture toward the large plate glass window with *O'Halloran's* painted in large green and gold letters.

"I'm Hennessy O'Halloran," the blonde cutie informs me.

Really?

That's when I dazzle her with my witty, eloquent repartee. "Uh…"

"You seem surprised by that, Mr. Pruitt," she says, cocking an eyebrow at me.

"Truitt," I correct her absently. "*You're* Hennessy O'Halloran?"

"Isn't that what I just said?"

"I'm sorry…I thought you were a—you know—a man…"

"Clearly," she replies, her lovely mouth quirking with some amusement.

Okay, this could go one of two ways. She's either a daughter or a niece, or—as is more common in L.A.—she's the obscenely young wife. Time to roll the dice.

"So, you're *Mrs.* O'Halloran then?" I venture.

I can see in an instant that I've just come up snake eyes.

"What? No!" she says with a surprised laugh. "I'm Jack's daughter."

I feel strangely relieved to hear that she's not the wife.

"Nice to meet you. I wonder if I might come inside and have a word with your father, then? I've traveled a very long way to see him."

She and the priest exchange a look that I can't quite decipher.

"You can deal with me, Mr. Truitt," she says, a little colder than just an instant ago.

"No, I'm sorry," I say, shaking my head. "Regrettably, this is something I can only discuss with the *owner*…"

"You're looking at her," she informs me flatly.

"Funny, you don't look like a Jack. But, then again, you don't look like a Hennessy, either," I snark.

Suddenly, her face hardens, and there's a brief, awkward beat of silence. Then she just turns around and goes back inside the pub without another word, leaving the good father and me to stare after her.

"I'm sorry. Did I say something?" I ask him quietly.

The priest pats my shoulder.

"Son, Jack O'Halloran died just after Christmas. Hennessy is his oldest girl, and she's running the place," he explains quietly.

"Oh God, I'm sorry," I say, then smack a hand over my mouth for taking the Lord's name in vain…again. "I'm sorry, Father, I didn't mean to…"

He offers me an amused smile and pulls the door open.

"No worries, son. Come on inside and warm your bones with a good stiff drink. I'm sure Hennessy will be happy to chat with you after that."

I nod absently and follow his direction. Dead? Well, I guess that explains the sudden radio silence on his end. But what that means for our deal…I have no clue.

Chapter Five

O'Halloran's Pub is dark. Dark paneling, dark wood floors. A huge, dark bar and matching dark barstools accented in dark burgundy. A half-dozen dark tables and chairs. And, all of these deeper hues might make the place depressing, it's actually quite the opposite. The atmosphere of the place is warm and welcoming—the perfect spot to get out of the cold and into the cozy. We're between lunch and dinner service right now, and there isn't another soul in the place when Bryan Truitt follows the father inside. I level my best disdainful look on him from behind the bar.

"I'm really sorry," he says sincerely. "Sorry for your loss and sorry for acting like a jerk—"

"You had business with my father?" I cut in coolly, not interested in his platitudes.

He nods.

"Well, it couldn't have been too important, seeing as how you didn't even know he was dead," I point out. Before he can reply, he's saved by a bit of divine intervention.

"Henny, love, how about a drink for our weary traveler, hmm? You can put it on my tab."

"Please, Father Romance," I begin.

"Father...*Romance*?" Truitt blusters.

A huge toothy grin from our local man of God.

"Nickname, son. I'm Father Grigory Romanski. I'm the rector at Basilica of St. Mary of the Assumption of the Blessed Virgin Mary of Mayhem."

Our guest snorts—though, I'm not sure if it's over the name of the church or the priest.

"What are you drinking?" Father Romance asks, unoffended.

"Uh...Stoli, please, neat."

I fix the drinks and set them out in front of the two men.

"What is that you're drinking?" Truitt asks, peering curiously into Father Romance's cocktail

"Ah, an oldie but a goodie! It's a Rye Presbyterian."

"What, don't you Catholics have your own drink? You have to borrow one from the Protestants?" he quips, and the two of them laugh.

I'm not so easily amused as I shoot some seltzer into a glass of my own and lean across the bar so I can get a good look at this guy's face when I speak to him. All in all, it's not a bad face. His jawline is well defined but not too angular. His nose has the slightest hint of a bump—a previous injury, perhaps? It's flanked by eyes the color of warm, golden-brown caramel. His hair is tousled but not in any organic way. There's some sort of product holding the thick, dark-brown strands perfectly in place. Oh yeah. This guy's got "Big City" written all over him.

"All right, Mr. Truitt. What, exactly, did you and my father have going?" I ask, not letting on that I'm already aware of his dealings with my dad.

He pulls a file folder from his briefcase and hands it to me. I open it and scan the pages, flipping quickly from one to the next. This all looks to be in line with the documentation I have back in the office.

"So he *was* going to sell the pub to you," I murmur.

"He was," he answers cautiously—clearly unsure of where he stands with me. I might understand a little of the densely worded pages I'm looking at, but then again, I might not. He bets on the latter. "We were just about to formalize the deal when your father…he…well, you know. But I assure you, Miss O'Halloran, everything is in order. This is a perfectly valid contract. I *suppose*—if you really wanted to spend the money—you *could* consult an attorney. But keep in mind that can be a considerable expense just to be told it's a done deal. I mean, I'm here. I've got the cash. Why don't you and I just finish what Jack and I started?"

He's confident and casual, one brow arched in a gesture that screams, "Go ahead, challenge me, I dare ya!"

I do dare, because I know better. Bryan Truitt may have an outstanding poker face, but he has absolutely no idea who he's playing against.

"So…you don't think I need to have an attorney look this over?" I ask innocently. "I mean, there's a lot of jargon here…" My brows furrow in concern as I scan the page in my hand.

His lips tip up into a placating smile that I might find offensive—if I didn't find it to be so…sad. He has no idea he's about to hang himself, so I just keep handing him the rope. I catch a glance of Father Romance out of the corner of my eye. He has a hand over his mouth to hide his smile.

"You know, I can just give you the gist of it. No reason to pay some bloodsucking ambulance chaser," Bryan says, rolling his eyes and shaking his head in disgust. "They'll just eat away at your father's estate until there's nothing left."

I set the papers down on the bar and look him straight in the eyes. Maybe I'd have gone easier on him if he hadn't just dropped my father into this. I take a long, deep breath and plaster a "sweet as pie" smile on my face.

"Well, you're just so…so *very* kind to be so concerned for me and my family."

"Ah, well, anything I can do to help you out at a difficult time like this," he replies, placing a reassuring hand over mine. It's warm and strong. "Hey, what do you say we find a notary, sign the paperwork, and I'll take you out for a nice dinner to celebrate."

Father Romance coughs now, trying to disguise a laugh. I slide my untouched glass of seltzer his way and return my concentration to Mr. Bryan Truitt, who still has his hand on mine.

"Oh, that's so tempting!" I exclaim. "But I'm afraid I have some work to do for my job. My real job. You see, I'm just in town long enough to get things settled here. Then it's back to Minneapolis for me."

"Oh ho! That's the big city around here, isn't it? And what does a lovely lady such as yourself do in a hustling, bustling metropolis such as Minneapolis? You aren't, by chance, a brain surgeon, are you?" he teases.

I throw back my head in an amused laugh.

"You're so funny," I gush. "No, actually, I have to review some case notes for my boss. I'm first chair on a big trial coming up."

I watch as his face goes ashen. Suddenly he's not looking so confident anymore.

"You're…you're a lawyer?" he asks, unable to disguise the gulp in his voice.

I smile brightly and nod.

"Yes, actually. I'm a Hennepin County public defender. So, no need to spend money on a bloodsucking ambulance chaser…because I *am* a bloodsucking ambulance chaser."

"I—I…I didn't know…" he stammers.

"Clearly," I say, my voice turning icy in a heartbeat. "Not having a very good time of it, are you, Mr. Truitt? You've come all this way only to find that my father is dead and his daughter is an attorney who actually understands everything in your proposed contract. I mean, what *are* the odds?"

"Henny…" Father Romance says softly. It's a warning—a caution that I shouldn't get carried away with my evisceration of the strong-jawed, weak-minded Bryan Truitt.

I extricate my hand from where it's still lodged under Truitt's and struggle to appear somewhat calm and professional in the face of his assumptions.

"Mr. Truitt, we both know that without my father's signature, this contract is invalid. And it'll remain that way unless and until the executor of his estate signs it. That would be me."

There. I've called his bluff, and I've won. I stare at his dumbfounded face, waiting for him to pack up his toys and go home. But that's not what he does. Bryan Truitt closes his gaping mouth, adjusts his tie, and takes a deep breath.

"Well then, Hennessy O'Halloran, what can I do to get you to sign on the dotted line?"

I give him a cross between a scoff and a snort.

"Nothing."

"I find that hard to believe. Everyone has a price. What will it take? Another ten percent on the purchase price? Twenty? How about twenty-five percent over market value?"

I stare at him incredulously. Something is very wrong here. This pub is priceless to my sisters and me, but the kind of money he's talking about is ridiculous considering the market right now.

"Why do you want this property so badly, Mr. Truitt?" I ask suspiciously.

He shrugs and smiles, much more confident than he was just a moment ago.

"Let's just say it's the perfect fit for one of my clients… and I've already invested a good deal of time and effort into this deal during my negotiations with your father. And, here's the thing—I'm a matchmaker, you see. I pair investors looking to expand into new territory with the ideal venue for their project. It's a win-win for the company and the community."

"And you," I point out.

"And me," he agrees. "So, what do you say, Miss O'Halloran? Want to make a match with me?"

I hold his gaze for a long beat before I speak again.

"I'm sorry, Mr. Truitt, but O'Halloran's is not for sale."

He seems to consider this for a second then rummages around in his briefcase for another paper. He pulls it out and studies it before talking again.

"Well, I hate to be the bearer of bad news, Miss O'Halloran—but if it's not for sale now, it will be very soon, according to the information I have. I believe the bank has called this loan, and you have less than six weeks left to make good. Otherwise, it goes to auction. The property will be sold to the highest bidder—which will be me—then the loan will be satisfied, and any remaining funds returned to you… after the trustee's cut and after all applicable fees have been deducted, of course. Trust me when I tell you there won't be enough cash left to use for the down payment on a new car, let alone a new building."

I feel the intense heat of my face flaming scarlet. Father Romance isn't chuckling anymore. In fact, he's looking very concerned as he puts a hand on Bryan's arm.

"Son, I think this might be a good time for you to have a walk around Mayhem—"

"No," I cut him off. "This would be a good time for him to get back in his car, drive to the airport, and go home to the land of sand and sunshine because there's *nothing* for him here."

Truitt hops off his barstool, grabs his briefcase, and flashes me a bright white, perfectly aligned smile. I'd like to slap it right off his face.

"Oh, I don't know about that, Miss O'Halloran. I've already spotted a couple of things I'd like to see right here in the quaint town of Mayhem. I think I'll hang around for a night or two. Maybe longer."

With that, he turns on his heel and walks out the front door, careful to go the long way around the snow bank this time.

Chapter Six

Bryan

Truttism Number 5: If you MUST put all your eggs in one basket then, for God's sake, don't count them till they're hatched!

I know I'm in trouble the minute I park the Lexus in front of the big Victorian on Chester Street. It's a plummy color with pink shutters and lots of the ornate spindles and window frames and decorative touches that I believe they call "gingerbread." At least the front walk is cleared down to the concrete so I don't have to worry about getting waylaid by a mound of grimy snow. I follow it up to the huge wrap-around porch, and I'm about to use the cat-shaped brass knocker when it's snatched out of my reach by the opening door.

"Oh! Hello, hello!" says a middle-aged woman with short white hair. She reminds me a little of Helen, actually, but much more pleasant.

"Uh... Hi, I'm Bryan Truitt. I think my assistant called

ahead for me?" I say, half hoping she tells me there's been a mistake and the place is all booked up. No such luck, though.

"Oh, you betcha!" She nods enthusiastically and waves me inside. "My name is Lucille van der Hoovenwald. But everyone just calls me Miss Lucy."

"Pleased to meet you, Miss Lucy," I respond to the back of her sweater vest as I follow her into what I can only describe as an old-fashioned parlor. It's got one of those big, velvet settees, and lamps with giant pink globes and long glass chimneys. Every surface is littered with figurines and teacups and tchotchkes galore.

"Wow, this is…some place you've got here," I say once we reach a giant cherry sideboard.

"Well, thank you, young man!" she replies with a smile, opening a drawer and then pressing a large brass-colored key into my hand.

"You're in the King Gustav room. It's right at the top of the stairs. You're the only guest, so please make yourself at home. There are snacks in the kitchen, and I'll have breakfast for you in the morning. Are you hungry now? I've got a chili corn-chip hotdish just coming out of the oven."

"Hot…dish?"

"Hotdish. All one word. Like a casserole, dear. I love a piping hotdish on a cold winter's night."

"Well, that's very sweet of you, but I think I might go out for a bite. Of course, I don't want to disturb you if I need to be out late for some reason."

"Oh, no worries. No worries at all. The front door is never locked. Just walk right in anytime, day or night. Just please be careful not to let the kitties out." She nods toward a pale pink chair with lace arm covers. I hadn't noticed the chair before. Or the cat curled up on it. Or the cat's sweater.

"Uh, Miss Lucy, is that cat wearing a *sweater*?" I ask, not quite trusting my travel-weary eyes.

She chuckles at me.

"Oh, you're just a funny one, aren't ya! You betcha, that there's my little Queen Elizabeth. She's usually in pink, don't ya know, but there was an unfortunate incident involving a hairball this morning, so she's borrowed that yellow one from her sister, Margaret Thatcher," she explains, then drops her voice. "*She's* sleeping with Winston Churchill in the den."

"Oh my!" I whisper in an appropriately scandalized tone.

"Indeed!" she agrees.

I'm laughing as I take my bag and climb the stairs in search of the King Gustav.

• • •

I usually make it a point to avoid any hotel without a five-star rating. That's not to say I haven't stayed in more humble accommodations. In those first years I was in business, I'd get in my car and drive across the country, from coast to coast, border to border. I often found myself at small roadside motels. The kind with towels as soft as sandpaper and bedspreads as clean as the men's room floor at Grand Central Station. But never, in my many pilgrimages, have I bunked at a place quite like the Pink Lady Slipper Inn of Mayhem, Minnesota.

One look at the weather forecast and Helen insisted I needed to stay someplace in town. She didn't want me navigating the icy back roads after dark…or after a few shots of vodka, for that matter. As I lie on the ruffled bedspread, looking up at the tin-tiled ceiling, I have to wonder if she didn't put me here just to get back at me for giving her a hard time yesterday morning.

For a second, I'd swear that the wallpaper is moving. The intricate latticework pattern of pink-budded flowers stretches from the ruby-red carpet up to the crown molding, and if I turn my head just so, they appear to wink at me. Yes. Wink.

They'll move in my peripheral vision, but not when I'm staring straight at them.

Creepy.

The bed itself is a cherry wood, queen-size four-poster with sheer panels hanging down around me. I'm sure it's meant to evoke an ethereal, romantic feel, but all I can think of is a bed somewhere in the Congo, shrouded in mosquito netting so you don't get dengue fever or malaria or some flesh-eating disease that makes you think the wallpaper is moving.

Also in the room are matching nightstands, a tall dresser, and one of those long oval mirrors in a wooden frame that stands on the floor. Oh, and there's lace. Lots and lots of lace. In fact, lace seems to be dripping off most surfaces in this house. Lace doilies. Lace curtains. Lace-covered lampshades and small lace pillows on every chair and couch. Even the guest registry is bound in a lace cover. I can practically feel my sperm count dropping as the testosterone is leached out of my body.

I sit up when I feel my phone vibrating from the pocket of my pants. A glance at the screen tells me it's Helen. A glance at my watch tells me she's getting ready to leave for the day.

"Hello, Helen."

"Well, hello, my Arctic explorer. How's that trench coat holding up? Are you nice and toasty?"

I groan into the receiver. She just laughs at me.

"Seriously, how's it going out there? I'm getting ready to head home for the night, and I was wondering if you need me to arrange that return ticket for tomorrow?"

"God, I hope so," I grumble. "But don't book it yet. Turns out Jack O'Halloran had a really good reason for not answering my calls."

"Oh? What's that?"

"He died."

"What? He *died*?"

"Uh-huh."

"Holy smokes!" she breathes out in shock. "What does that mean for your deal?"

"I'm not sure yet. Turns out the daughter's managing the estate. She just found out about the deal a couple of days ago. I showed her the contract, but, of course, it isn't signed."

"And what did she say?" I can tell that Helen is hanging on every word. This must sound like one of those daytime soaps she likes so much.

"At first I thought I could convince her it was already a done deal. But, it turns out she's a *lawyer*."

A snort of laughter from Helen. "Serves you right, trying to take advantage of a grieving woman."

"Yeah, well, I pretty much got my butt handed to me. But I won't make the mistake of underestimating Miss Hennessy O'Halloran again."

"That's her name? Hennessy? Like the whiskey?" Helen asks incredulously.

"Oh, wow… You know, I hadn't even thought about that. Makes sense, her father running a pub and all." I chuckle. "Anyway, with a little luck, I'll have this wrapped up tomorrow afternoon and be on a flight tomorrow night."

"Hmmm… Don't forget about Truittism Number Five. Eggs, basket, chickens, and all that," she reminds me.

"Score another one for Helen," I say with mock spirit.

"Yeah, well, I have a feeling your last assistant didn't memorize your quirky canon of witticism," she throws at me. "What was her name? Whitney? Courtney? Sidney?"

"Brittany," I correct her. "Her name was Brittany, and she took great dictation…"

"Uh-huh. I'll just bet she did."

I hear the smile in Helen's voice, and it's suddenly very irritating. "Helen, did you know that there are like a hundred people applying for every open job in this country right now? Maybe it's not such a great idea to torment your boss, lest he hires one of the ninety-nine in line behind you," I remind her, only half teasing.

"Well, that's just perfect because it'll take ninety-nine people to do what I do for you," she slams back at me.

She's right. I know it, and she knows I know it, so there's no sense pretending otherwise. I sigh my resignation.

"You know what, Helen, you're right. When I get back, I'm taking you out for a nice lunch somewhere."

"Oh, now, wouldn't that be a treat!" she says with pleased surprise. "Well, okay, then, I'm just going to head home now. You call me if you need me."

"I will," I assure her, because I can't manage without my personal little troll doll.

She knows it, and I know she knows it.

Chapter Seven

HENNESSY

"Oh for God's sake, what are you holding out for? Just sell it already," Win says through a mouthful of steak.

"Sell it?" Jameson squeaks at her husband. "The pub is older than we are. It was our parents' dream…"

"Then your father should've taken more care with it, don't you think?" he challenges.

What. A. Jerk.

I think about how satisfying it would be to wrap my hands around his neck. But I don't think Jameson would let me do it in front of Jackson. Or Win's father, Big Win, for that matter. Dinner at my sister's house is, perhaps, not the best place to contemplate murdering my brother-in-law. Instead, I take a deep, slow breath and will my pounding pulse to settle.

"Hennessy," Win says, sending me into tachycardia again, "if you take the deal this guy…what's his name?"

"Truitt," I grit out. "Bryan. Truitt."

"Right. If you take the deal this Truitt guy is offering,

you can pay off the loan and have cash left over. Bailey's got college next year, too, don't forget."

How could I? That's been one of my biggest concerns since this all blew up. I consider the jerk carefully. He's not wrong. For once.

"You make some really good points," I say begrudgingly.

He nods as if to affirm what he's known all along.

"But Mama and Pops worked their whole lives for that place. There must be another way," Jameson interjects.

Win turns toward his wife and cocks an eyebrow.

"And who, exactly, is going to run the pub, even if you do manage to find the money? You've got the baby, Bailey's in high school, Walker's in college…"

"What about me?" I pipe up before I can stop myself. "I could run it."

"Last time I checked, Hennessy, you don't live here. So how are you planning on helping out?" Win's question isn't so much curiosity as a challenge. "Or were you thinking you'd play barkeep for a little while and then run away back to your real life—your real job—when you get tired of doing inventory and washing glasses?"

I'm about to respond to his snarkiness when his father intervenes in the most unexpected manner.

"Enough!"

We all jump at the uncharacteristically harsh sound of Big Win's voice…and then we all gawk at him. Even little Jackson has put down his fistful of mashed potatoes to look up at his grandfather with wide, green eyes.

"Dad, you don't need to get involved in their family business," Win says, assuming that his father is frustrated by Jameson and me. But my brother-in-law has assumed wrong.

"Winston," Big Win begins, "Jameson and Hennessy *are* family, and you'd do well to remember that, son. And considering you just took over my law practice not six months

ago, I'm surprised you can't empathize with the dilemma your wife and her sisters are facing."

Holy. Crap.

Winston Clarke, Sr., is a big, beefy man with a fringe of hair around the sides of his head and a bald spot up top. He's a man of very few words. You'd think that might be a problem for an attorney. Not for him. For forty years he used it to his advantage, wielding awkward silence in the courtroom like a ninja might wield a sword. Now, Win the younger's eyes drop down to his half-eaten plate of food as two bright scarlet patches form on his cheeks. He doesn't respond to his father's words.

"Hennessy," Big Win says, catching my eye across the table. "Win is rude and inconsiderate...but he's not wrong. It's easy to say 'keep the bar open' until you think about *how* to keep it open. I'm not saying it's impossible; I'm just suggesting you take some time to consider the reality of this situation. Your father was a good man, a dedicated man. That pub was his life, apart from you girls and your mother. But, as much as I'm sure he'd love to see you carry on, he'd never want you to suffer for it."

"Thank you, sir." I give him a respectful nod and watch as he gets to his feet.

"Dad, you're not leaving already, are you?" Jameson asks her father-in-law.

"Afraid so, my dear. This old man's going ice fishing tomorrow, and I mean to be on the road before dawn."

He leans over to give Jackson a kiss on the head.

"Goppa!" my nephew exclaims happily.

Big Win says his good-byes and then makes his way through the living room and out the front door.

"*We* could do it," Jameson says, so quietly that I think I've misheard her.

"What are you talking about?" I ask.

"We could pay off the loan. Like investors...taking repayments once the pub starts to turn a profit again."

Win puts his fork down and narrows his eyes at his wife. "We *who*?"

"We! You and I. *Us*, Win. It's not like we don't have the money."

"Oh my God!" I gasp, suddenly excited by the prospect. "That could work!"

"No."

Win utters the single word with such finality that I feel as if I'm watching a father with his wayward daughter.

"I'm sorry...*no*?" she echoes incredulously.

"That's right, Jameson. No. It's my family's money. Money *I* earn. I will not let you throw it out the window to support some failing dive money pit."

I cannot believe he just said that, and apparently, neither can my sister, who's gone very still. Suddenly, I feel as if I'm in the eye of a storm, where an unsettling calm lies while tumultuous destruction roars all around.

"Hennessy, please excuse us. Win and I are going to speak in the kitchen for a moment."

"What? But I'm not done eating..." he whines.

One sharp look from my sister and he's throwing his fork down on the dining room table to follow her.

I get up and move to the chair that Big Win vacated, next to Jackson. He's looking up at me with that beautiful little cherub face. I pull him out of the high chair and put him on my lap.

"Hey there, sweet boy," I say, bouncing him on my knee. He smiles, but he's not his usual playful self. It's not hard to understand why—the tension in this house is thick enough to cut with a knife.

I can hear snippets of what sounds to be a very intense, hushed conversation not fifty feet away from me. It's not that

I want to listen. In fact, I'm suddenly wishing I'd taken Big Win's cue and left early. I don't like seeing Jameson like this—under the thumb of a man for whom she gave up her career. Whose child she raises and whose meals she cooks while he's out shagging half of Mayhem. I'd like to say that last part is just speculation, but dipstick isn't especially discreet in his extracurricular activities, clearly believing Jameson to be too dim to figure it out. And, while Jameson is a lot of things, dim is not one of them. She knows full well what he's up to… though why she doesn't leave him is a mystery to us all.

"…*since when?*" I hear Jameson hiss. Then I lose most of his reply, but I do catch the end of it.

"…*And if you don't like it, you know where the door is.*"

That's followed by loud stomping through the other side of the house and up the stairs. I look down at the baby, who's using his chubby fingers as chew toys.

"Come on, little man. Let's go see how Mommy's doing," I murmur as I stand up and seat him on my hip. When we walk into the kitchen, Jameson is bent over the sink, bracing herself against the counter as she shakes with silent sobs. "Oh, James!" I rush to her and pat her back gently. "It's going to be okay. Don't you worry about it…"

"No," she sniffs, turning to face us. "No, it's not going to be okay. It's never going to be okay because I'm married to a horrible human being, Henny."

I'm not sure how to respond to that. She's right. And I'm not going to blow smoke up her apron just to make her feel better about the creep she's hitched her wagon to.

Little Jackson reaches out for his mother.

"Maaaammaaaa…" he gurgles.

Jameson abruptly stops crying, wipes her tears with the back of her hand, and pulls her son into her arms.

"Hello, my love," she coos into his ear as he snuggles in to rest his head on her shoulder. "Don't you worry, baby boy.

Mama's going to take care of everything." She puts a hand on my forearm and gives it a gentle squeeze. "We'll figure this out. I wish I could say Win will come around, but that's not very likely, I'm afraid."

"What a douche," I mutter under my breath.

"Hennessy, language, please!" Jameson squawks at me.

"Oh, please. The kid isn't paying any attention," I assure her. It's at that very second that the imp pulls his head off his mother's shoulder, smiles brightly, and yells.

"Doosh! Doosh, Mama! Dooooosh!"

"Yeah…I'll just let myself out," I say, gathering my coat and getting out the door as fast as I can.

Chapter Eight

BRYAN

Truittism Number 4: Get to know your enemy; otherwise, you're bound to get your back end handed to you when you least expect it.

I'm sitting up in bed, working on my laptop when I hear the tentative knock at my door.

"Mr. Truitt? It's Miss Lucy. Are you still awake in there?"

Well, if I wasn't before, I certainly would be now.

"Uh, yes, Miss Lucy," I call, jumping up and out of bed in my briefs and T-shirt. "Did you need something?"

"You have a phone call."

A phone call? Here? No one but Helen knows where I am, and she'd ring the cell phone if she wanted to reach me. Unless…

"Uh…just a second…" I grab a pair of workout shorts from my roller bag and slip them on. When I finally open the door, she holds out a cordless handset for me.

"You can bring it down with you in the morning. I have another one charging in the kitchen."

"Thank you," I say with a brief smile as I take it from her and close the door behind me. "Hello?"

"Mr. Truitt."

Oh my God. It's *her*.

"Miss O'Halloran. How did you know I was here?"

"There are only two places to stay in town, and I happen to know that the Mayhem Motel is full-up with ice fishermen this week."

"So you deduced I'd be at Pink Fuzzy Slipper Inn."

I hear a distinct snort of laughter from her end of the line.

"I think you mean the *Pink Lady Slipper Inn*. Pink Lady Slipper is the Minnesota state flower. And yes, I deduced, but Father Romance mentioned it as well."

"How did he know?"

"He knows everything that goes on in this town," she informs me.

"Okay…well, as much as I'd love to pass the hours discussing flowers and fathers, I'm curious as to the nature of this call. Have you rethought my offer?"

"Hardly," she mutters disdainfully. "No, I'm just calling to reiterate that you should go home tomorrow. The pub will not be available for purchase, and I'd hate for you to waste your time here in Mayhem when you could be destroying someone else's quaint little town."

My turn to snort.

"Been googling, have we?"

"Oh yes, Mr. Truitt. I particularly liked the article titled BRYAN TRUITT WAGES WAR ON SMALL-TOWN AMERICA."

"You shouldn't believe everything you read, Miss O'Halloran," I suggest amiably. "I've been welcomed by more communities than I can count—but they're not running to the newspapers about it."

"Really." The single word isn't so much of a question as an accusation. She thinks I'm lying to her.

"Really. Next time you're near a computer, look up Middleman, Idaho, and Ranier, Montana. They were quite happy with the influx of cash and jobs that my company brought to their communities. Communities that'd been struggling—boarded up storefronts, foreclosed homes, unemployed workers—now thriving."

She harrumphs, and suddenly I'm struck by the desire to hear her laugh. For real. No snarky snorts or disbelieving chuckles. For some reason, I suspect Hennessy O'Halloran's laughter will be sweet and light, like the sound of tinkling bells on a wind chime.

What the hell, Bryan?

"Yes, well," she begins, interrupting my bizarre reverie, "be that as it may, this community neither wants nor needs your services."

"That remains to be seen," I counter, and I can feel the rage ratcheting up from her side of the phone.

"I assure you, it does not, Mr. Truitt," she spits at me.

From sweet bells to hissing harpy in less than five seconds. Impressive.

"Miss O'Halloran, why are you making this so adversarial? Your father and I had many a pleasant conversation about this. Clearly it was his intention—his wish—to sell the pub and cash out."

I hear her suck in a deep breath. I'm trying. God knows I'm trying. But she's making it hard.

"Yeah, well, that's when he didn't want us to know what was going on with his finances. Now we know. And now we intend to do something about it," she informs me coolly.

"Oh? And what do you plan to do—get a loan? Cash in your retirement plan? Oh, wait, you're a public defender, right? You probably don't have a retirement plan…" I realize that I'm sounding nasty, so I pause and reset, coming back with a softer, conspiratorial approach. "C'mon, Hennessy, you're a smart woman. You know what I'm offering is a good deal. There are other, less scrupulous developers who'd come in here and rip it out of your hands."

There is a long, tense silence.

"Good night, Mr. Truitt," she grits out at last and hangs up the phone on me.

"Good night, Hennessy," I murmur to the dial tone.

. . .

I have to admit, Miss Lucy puts on a better breakfast spread than any hotel I've ever stayed at. Fresh fruit along with light and fluffy pancakes and crispy bacon are served up as soon as I come downstairs.

"Wow. This coffee is amazing," I murmur appreciatively into my mug.

"Oh, nonsense," she says skeptically, taking a seat across from me at the table. "I'm sure a man like you has had plenty of coffee in places like France and Italy and Costa Rica."

"Well, maybe," I agree. "But this is, by far, the best cup I've ever had on American soil."

She doesn't comment, but I catch the flush of pride that washes over her soft, well-creased face.

"So, what are your plans for today, Mr. Truitt? And should I expect the pleasure of your company again tonight?"

I hold up a finger while I swallow a mouthful of the pancakes.

"No offense, Miss Lucy, but I hope not. I'd like to be on a plane home tonight. But I can't leave until I settle some business here."

"O'Halloran's?"

Christ, does everyone know everything in this town?

"Uh…yes, actually," I say with a nod, as I tuck into